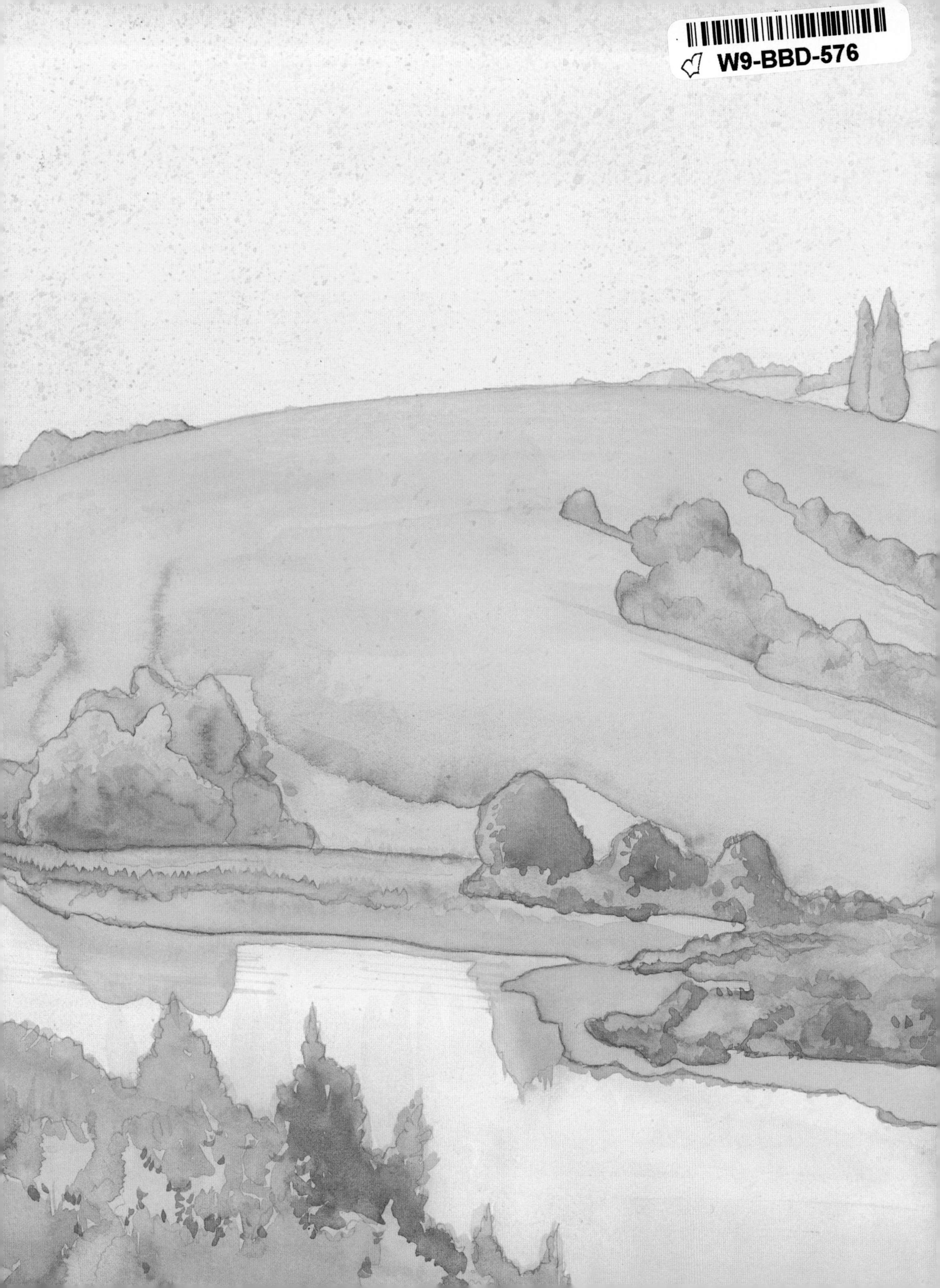

The Classic Treasury of Aesop's Fables

THE CLASSIC TREASURY OF

AESOP'S FABLES

Illustrated by Don Daily

RP KIDS
CLASSICS
PHILADELPHIA · LONDON

To my son, Joe.

19   18   17   16   15   14

Digit on the right indicates the number of this printing.

Library of Congress Cataloging-in-Publication Number 98-72363

ISBN 978-0-7624-2876-2

Illustrated by Don Daily
Designed by Frances J. Soo Ping Chow
Edited by Caroline E. Tiger
Typography: Fairfield

Running Press Book Publishers
2300 Chestnut Street
Philadelphia, Pennsylvania 19103-4371

Visit us on the web!
www.runningpress.com/kids

Contents

Introduction 6

The Crow and the Pitcher 9

The Fox and the Grapes 10

The City Mouse and the Country Mouse 13

The Swallow and the Crow 19

The Ass and the Grasshopper 20

The Gnat and the Bull 23

The Goose Who Laid the Golden Eggs 24

The Mouse and the Frog 27

The Monkey and the Camel 28

The Fox and the Mask 31

The Cat and the Bell .32

The Bull and the Bullfrog 35

The Stag and His Antlers 36

The Dog and His Reflection 39

The Fox and the Crow 40

The Tortoise and the Hare 43

The Lion and the Mouse 47

The Ass, the Fox, and the Lion 50

The Birds, the Beasts, and the Bat 53

The Frogs Who Desired a King 54

Introduction

Welcome to a world where anything can happen and anything does—a bullfrog blows up so big that he bursts, a tortoise races a hare, a goose lays golden eggs. . . . But if Aesop's world is so out of the ordinary, why do some of the characters seem so familiar?

Because Aesop's fables are not only fun and silly—they're just like real life! This is why they have lasted hundreds and hundreds of years. And at the end of each tale is a moral, or a statement that the fable has shown to be true—a kind of rule to live by. There are some very famous morals inside this book, including "Slow and steady wins the race," "To each his own," and "Be yourself." Generations upon generations have heeded these wise words—and so can you.

So turn the page and leap into the world of Aesop—it's waiting for you!

The Crow
and the Pitcher

A crow, after flying many miles, became terribly thirsty. She searched everywhere for a place to drink but found nothing. Just when she was losing hope, she discovered a pitcher with a few inches of water in it.

"At last," she said, "I'm saved."

She tried to take a sip of the water, but her beak was too short and the pitcher was too narrow. She considered the problem for a long time.

"If I break the pitcher or knock it over, the water will spill and I'll be no better off than before. There must be a solution."

Then she recalled a birdbath that was full after a rain. She remembered how the water overflowed the rim of the bath every time another bird landed in it.

"Eureka!" she said. "That's my solution!" She began gathering pebbles and dropping them into the pitcher. With each pebble she added, the level of the water rose slightly. Soon the water was high enough for her to drink. Refreshed, she happily continued her journey.

WITH A LITTLE PLANNING YOU CAN GAIN
WHAT AT FIRST SEEMS IMPOSSIBLE.

The Fox
and the Grapes

A fox was wandering down a country lane one day when she noticed some grapes growing over an arbor. One bunch was especially attractive: the grapes were as big as a cow's eyes and as purple as midnight. They glistened with morning dew. The fox, never missing a chance to eat, thought these juicy-looking gems would make a fine breakfast.

"Hmm . . ." she thought, "those grapes are tempting, but they're so high up. I don't know how I'll ever reach them."

She paced back and forth for a few moments. She tried leaping into the air and grabbing them with her teeth. She tried climbing the arbor. Always the grapes were beyond her grasp.

Giving up, she snarled, "Oh, those grapes aren't worth my trouble. They look sour."

IT'S EASY TO SPEAK BADLY OF THINGS YOU CAN'T HAVE.

The City Mouse
and the Country Mouse

The city mouse hadn't seen his country cousin in a long while, so he decided to pay a visit.

"Welcome! Welcome!" said the country mouse when his cousin arrived. "How fine you look in your tailored suit. I do hope you packed something more comfortable, though. I'm afraid this barn that I live in gets dusty."

"Indeed," said the city mouse, brushing a piece of straw from his sleeve. "How do you ever put up with all this dried grass?"

"I like my home just as it is," replied the country mouse. "All this soft, warm straw makes it cozy. But you must be hungry after your trip. I've prepared a special meal."

"Wonderful!" said the city mouse. "As a matter of fact, I am a bit hungry."

The country mouse went to work setting the table. He brought out sunflower seeds, dandelion greens, an apple core, two walnut shells filled with fresh milk, and cornbread crumbs. He was especially proud of the cornbread crumbs, because they were so hard to come by. He had had to sneak into the farmhouse and risk being smacked with a broom. He hated when that happened, but he wanted to impress his cousin with his fine food.

The city mouse wasn't impressed. In fact, he didn't care for the meal at all.

"My poor cousin!" said the city mouse, "How can you live on such simple foods? You should come with me to the city. I'll show you what fine dining really is."

"I'll admit that my diet is plain," said the country mouse, "but I like it just the same."

"But," the city mouse replied, "you don't know what you're missing."

The two mice sat and talked for a while, and then it was time for bed. The country mouse fell asleep right away. The city mouse tossed and turned.

"What's that noise?" asked the city mouse, annoyed.

"Huh? What noise?" replied the country mouse, yawning.

"That horrible screeching sound," said the city mouse. "Can't you hear it?"

"Oh! You mean the crickets! They're just crickets—you get used to them. It's a soothing kind of sound, don't you think?"

"Not me!" replied the city mouse, but his cousin had already fallen back to sleep.

The city mouse continued to toss and turn. When he finally dozed off, a rooster began to crow, announcing the arrival of morning.

"Rise and shine, Cousin," said the country mouse. "Are you ready for breakfast?"

"Cousin," answered the city mouse, "this country living isn't to my liking. I want to go back to the city as soon as I can. Why don't you come with me and see what it's like?"

"I'd love that!" said the country mouse, very excited.

So after breakfast, the two set out for the city.

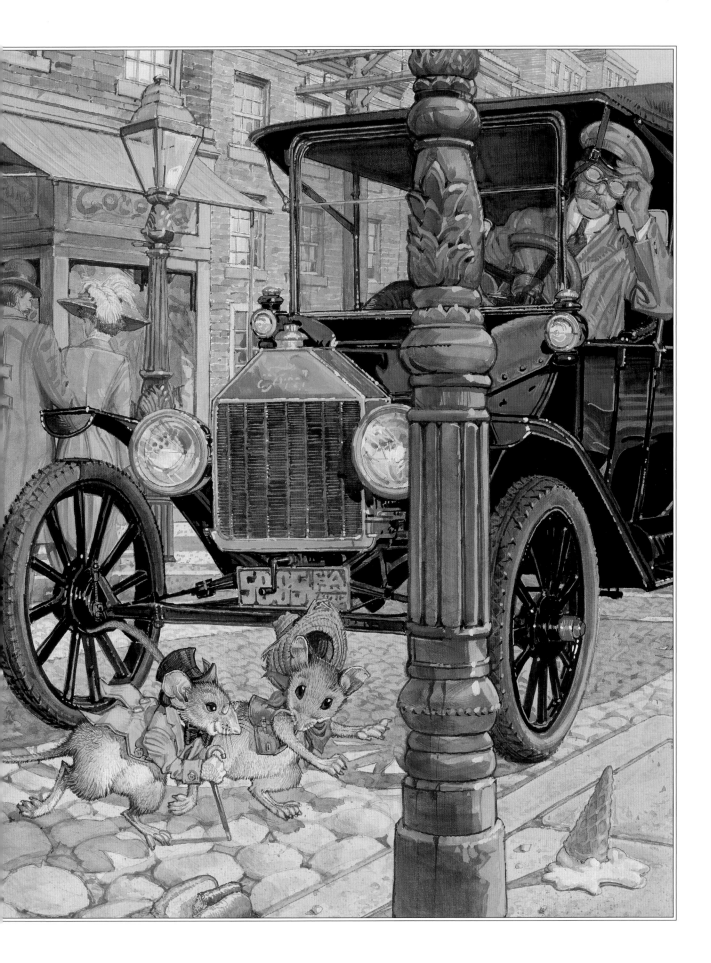

They arrived late in the afternoon. The country mouse was impressed by the carpets and woodwork in his cousin's apartment. After resting a few minutes, they decided it was time for dinner.

"What would you like to eat?" asked the city mouse. "The city is full of fine restaurants. I know a good Dumpster behind a seafood place, but you have to eat quickly because there are lots of cats around. Or perhaps we can pick up something on the street. Sometimes children drop their ice cream cones, or people toss away the ends of their hot dog buns."

"Oh! Ice cream? Hot dog buns? I don't know what you're talking about, but it all sounds so wonderful! Let's go out and explore."

It was rush hour when the mice reached the street. People filled the sidewalks, and traffic clogged the avenues. The mice darted between shoes, dashed around automobiles, and scurried along curbs.

"Isn't this exciting?" said the city mouse.

"I'm afraid I don't much care for it," replied the country mouse as he unstuck his leg from a wad of bubble gum on the sidewalk. "It's dangerous, and it smells bad."

"What?" said the city mouse, who couldn't hear over the noise from a passing bus.

"I want to go back to your apartment," said the country mouse.

When the mice returned to the apartment, a party was going on. There was a table set up with all kinds of cakes, fruits, and cheeses.

"We're in luck," said the city mouse. "As soon as the party's over, we'll feast on the leftovers."

They hid for several hours until the last guest went home.

"Now's our chance," exclaimed the city mouse, and he and his cousin climbed up the tablecloth to explore the banquet.

The country mouse was fascinated by a huge piece of chocolate cake. He especially enjoyed munching on the sugar frosting rose, and he even found the candle to be tasty. Next he joined his cousin in devouring a bit of cheese.

"This really is a treat," he said between bites.

All at once, the door swung open and a huge dog bounded into the dining room. It ran around the table, barking and yelping and causing quite a fuss. The two mice barely made their way back to safety.

Out of breath and still shaking, the country mouse said to the city mouse, "Cousin, you may enjoy the fine food and fast pace of the city, but I'd rather have my simple meals in peace and quiet."

And saying that, the country mouse went home.

TO EACH HIS OWN.

The Swallow and
the Crow

The swallow and the crow had an argument as to
which was the finer bird. The crow ended the dispute by saying,
"Your feathers may be beautiful and fine during the summer, but
mine will protect me and last for many winters."

The Ass and
the Grasshopper

After hearing some grasshoppers chirping, an ass was enchanted by their music and wanted to acquire the same melodic charms. When he asked them what they ate to sing so sweetly, they told him that they dined on nothing but dew. Consequently, the ass followed the same diet, but he soon died of hunger.

ONE PERSON'S MEAT IS ANOTHER'S POISON.

The Gnat
and the Bull

After a gnat had been buzzing around the head of a bull for several minutes, he finally settled down upon a horn and begged the bull's pardon for disturbing him. "If my weight causes you any inconvenience at all," he said, "just tell me, and I'll be off in a moment."

"Oh, don't trouble your mind about that," said the bull. "It's all the same to me whether you go or stay. To tell you the truth, I didn't even know you were there."

THE SMALLER THE MIND, THE GREATER THE CONCEIT.

23

The Goose Who Laid the Golden Eggs

A farmer and his wife were barely getting by on the money they earned selling eggs and butter. Then a miracle happened. The wife was collecting eggs from the hens and geese when she noticed that one egg was particularly heavy. When she examined it, she found it to be made of solid gold.

"We're rich!" she cried as she ran to show her husband.

Every few days, the goose would lay another golden egg, and soon the farmer and his wife were wearing expensive clothes, building onto their farm, and hiring servants. But for every golden egg the goose laid, the couple would spend two eggs' worth of gold.

One day, they realized that they owed everyone money.

"I know," said the farmer, "let's cut open the goose and take out all the gold at once!"

"Good idea," said his wife, "Here's the knife—you do it."

The farmer wasted no time catching the goose and slaughtering it. But when he cut it open, he found it to be just an ordinary goose.

GREED DESTROYS THE SOURCE OF GOOD.

The Mouse and
the Frog

On an ill-fated day a mouse made the acquaintance of a frog, and they set off on their travels together. The frog pretended to be very fond of the mouse and invited him to visit the pond in which he lived.

To keep his companion out of harm's way, the frog tied the mouse's front foot to his own hind leg, and thus they proceeded for some distance by land. When they came to the pond, the frog told the mouse to trust him and be brave as he began swimming across the water. But, no sooner had they reached the middle of the pond than the frog suddenly plunged to the bottom, dragging the unfortunate mouse after him.

Now the struggling and floundering mouse made such a great commotion in the water that he managed to attract the attention of a hawk, who pounced upon the mouse and carried him away to be devoured. Since the frog was still tied to the mouse, he shared the same fate as his companion and was justly punished for his treachery.

IF YOU PLOT THE DOWNFALL OF YOUR NEIGHBOR,
YOU OFTEN WILL BE BETRAYED BY YOUR OWN TREACHERY.

The Monkey and the Camel

At a great meeting of the beasts, the monkey stood up to dance, and his performance delighted all those present so much that they honored him with great applause. This praise infuriated the envious camel, who stood and tried to show up the monkey with his own dancing. But the camel made such a fool of himself that the beasts shook their heads and drove him out of the meeting with their jeers and laughter.

BE YOURSELF.

The Fox
and the Mask

A fox had stolen into the house of an actor, and as he was rummaging among the actor's possessions, he found a remarkable mask that was a fine imitation of a human head.

"What a fine looking head!" he cried. "Pity that it lacks brains!"

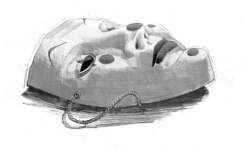

The Cat
and the Bell

A group of mice was sitting in a hayloft, discussing the problem of the farmer's cat.

"With that cat around, it's not safe to step outside anymore," said one mouse.

"We need to find a way to tell when the cat's around and when she isn't," said another.

Many plans were discussed and rejected. Finally, one mouse announced what he thought to be the perfect solution.

"The problem with the cat is that she's so quiet," said the mouse. "What if we tie a small bell around her neck so that every time she moves, the bell will tinkle? That way, we'll always know where she is, and she'll never be able to surprise us."

"Brilliant!" said one mouse.

"Perfect!" said another.

"What a wonderful plan!" exclaimed a third.

All agreed that putting a bell on the cat was the solution they were looking for. When they finished congratulating one another, the oldest mouse spoke up:

"Putting a bell on the cat sounds like a good idea, but tell me, which one of us will do the job?"

It's easy to think of impossible solutions.

The Bull
and the Bullfrog

A young bullfrog was exploring the far end of the pond, when a bull walked up for a drink of water. The bullfrog was amazed by the bull's size. He had never seen anything so large before. Excited, he swam home to tell his father what he had seen.

"Father, I saw the most gigantic animal in the world," said the young bullfrog. "He was at the other end of the pond."

"Now, son," his father replied, "everyone knows that I'm the biggest animal in this pond. Just watch me."

The old bullfrog took in a big gulp of air and puffed himself up.

"Was that animal bigger than this?" his father asked.

"Much bigger than that," said his son.

"How about now?" asked the father, puffing himself even bigger.

"I'm afraid he was much bigger still," said the son.

"Well," said the father bullfrog, as he sucked in as much air as he could, "he couldn't have been much bigger than this."

"But he really was much bigger than that," replied the young bullfrog.

"Okay, son, watch me now. He couldn't possibly have been bigger than this."

The old bullfrog began to puff himself up even more when suddenly—BANG! He burst into tiny pieces.

STRETCH YOUR ARM NO FARTHER THAN YOUR SLEEVE WILL REACH.

The Stag
and His Antlers

A stag stopped beside a pond to gaze at his reflection in the water.

"What splendid antlers!" he exclaimed. "They're so large and elegant. Nobody has a more beautiful set of antlers than I."

As the stag continued to study his reflection, he noticed his legs.

"These awful legs!" he moaned. "How long and thin and silly they look. Such knobby knees! Why can't my legs be as shapely as my antlers?"

Just then, the stag heard dogs barking in the distance.

"Hunters!" he cried. "And they're getting closer. I'd better get away from here."

The stag leaped into the safety of the woods. He hadn't gotten far when his antlers became tangled in some thorny bushes. The more he struggled, the more tangled the stag became. Meanwhile, the dogs drew nearer.

"This is the end of me!" thought the stag. But at that instant, his antlers came untangled and he bounded away to safety.

"What a fool I am," the stag thought. "The antlers I thought were so wonderful almost killed me, and the legs I disliked so much saved me."

BEAUTY IS NOT AS IMPORTANT AS USEFULNESS.

The Dog
and His Reflection

A dog who thought he was very clever stole a steak from a butcher shop. As he ran off with it in his teeth, he crossed a bridge that spanned a small, still river.

As he looked over the side of the bridge and into the water, he saw his own reflection, but he thought it was another dog.

"Hmm," thought the dog, "that other dog has a nice, juicy steak almost as good as the one I have. He's a stupid-looking dog. If I can scare him, perhaps he'll drop his steak and run."

This seemed to the dog to be a perfect plan. But as he opened his mouth to bark, he dropped his steak into the water and lost it.

The Fox
and the Crow

A fox spied a crow sitting on a branch of a tall tree with a golden piece of cheese in her beak. The fox, who was both clever and hungry, quickly thought of a plan to get the cheese away from the crow.

Pretending to notice the crow for the first time, the fox exclaimed, "My, what a beautiful bird! I must say that is the most elegant black plumage I have ever seen. Look how it shines in the sun. Simply magnificent!"

The crow was flattered by all this talk about her feathers. She listened to every sugary word the fox spoke.

The fox continued, "I must say that this is the most beautiful bird in the world. But I wonder, can such a stunning bird have an equally splendid voice? That," said the cunning fox, "would be too much to ask."

The crow, wanting the fox to hear her voice, opened her beak to let out an ear-piercing "CAW!" As she did so, the cheese tumbled out of her mouth and was gobbled up instantly by the fox.

NEVER TRUST A FLATTERER.

The Tortoise and the Hare

The hare couldn't understand how the tortoise ever accomplished anything.

"Tell me, tell me!" demanded the hare as he hopped circles around the tortoise. "How do you get things done? You move so slowly that you hardly move at all. Just look at me—look at me—I cover lots of ground every day."

To prove it, the hare sprinted across the field and back again before the tortoise could open his mouth.

"Well . . ." began the tortoise as he considered his answer, "it's like this . . . First of all, I find it much better to plan ahead and then—"

"No time for this! No time!" interrupted the hare. And in a flash, he was gone. A few days later, the hare happened to meet the tortoise on a mossy rock.

"Hey there, Mr. Tortoise!" shouted the hare, appearing suddenly and giving the tortoise a terrible scare. "If you don't watch out, somebody's going to make soup of you."

"Oh," replied the tortoise, poking his head out of his shell, "you're just mocking me. Besides . . . I don't believe—"

But the hare was impatient:

"I think what you need is some exercise. It'll start your heart pumping. It'll get your blood moving. Try it! You'll see! You'll see!"

"Exercise?" said the tortoise. "Let me think a moment . . . Hmm . . . By exercise, do you mean—"

"A race!" blurted the hare. "I challenge you to a race."

And before the tortoise could reply, the date was set.

On the morning of the race, everyone turned out to witness the contest of the season. The owl had selected a fair course the night before, and the lion and the frog agreed to judge the race and announce the winner.

The tortoise and the hare stood side by side at the starting line. The race was about to begin. The crowd held its breath. A crow, sitting in a nearby tree, dropped a twig, signaling the start. When the twig hit the ground, the racers were off.

The shouts and croaks and caws and barks of the crowd were deafening, but the hare was already too far ahead to hear them. The tortoise moved along as fast as he could, which is to say, not very fast at all. But soon he, too, was well away from the starting line.

When the hare reached the halfway mark, he turned to look behind him. The tortoise was nowhere in sight. It was almost lunch time, and the hare thought about making a salad to celebrate his certain victory. He went off in search of carrots and lettuce and whatever else he might find.

Meanwhile, the tortoise plodded along, slowly closing the gap between himself and the hare. The whole time he kept in his mind the thought of crossing the finish line.

The hare had gathered a huge amount of salad greens for his victory salad, and even went to the trouble of finding tender blossoms. When he had finished the last of his lunch, he returned to the track and dashed a little farther ahead. But the sun was high and hot, and the hare was drowsy from such a big meal. Once again he left the track, this time in search of some shade.

Little did he know that the tortoise was behind him, just around the bend.

"There's one thing I have to give the tortoise credit for," thought the hare as he drifted off to sleep. "Since he carries his house with him, he can get shade whenever he wants."

The tortoise pressed onward, not even realizing that he was passing the hare. "He's nowhere in sight," the tortoise thought, "but the race isn't over until it's over."

Like the hare, the tortoise was also feeling tired from the sun, but he kept his goal in mind. "One thing I have to give the hare credit for," he said to himself. "At least he doesn't have to carry his home with him wherever he goes. No wonder he can move so fast."

The tortoise kept moving, and the hare dreamed about victory.

A while later, the tortoise began to hear the friendly sounds of animals chirping, cawing, and growling, and he realized that he was nearing the finish line. As he cleared the top of a hill, he could see the crowd at the bottom. The crowd saw him, too, and began to cheer.

In his dreams, the hare thought the cheers were for him, but suddenly he awoke and realized the race was not yet won. He jumped up and dashed for the finish line. He reached the top of the last hill just in time to see the tortoise win.

SLOW AND STEADY WINS THE RACE.

The Lion and
the Mouse

A mouse was wandering through the jungle, not paying any attention to where he was going. Suddenly he realized that he had climbed onto the back of a huge, sleeping lion.

"Uh-oh," the mouse thought as he tried to slowly tiptoe off. The lion, tickled by the mouse's feet, reached up to scratch. When he felt the mouse, he awakened.

"What's this?" roared the lion as he grabbed the trembling creature.

Slowly he lifted the mouse to his mouth. The poor mouse could see the lion's sharp teeth and feel his hot breath as he was pulled closer and closer.

"Please sir," squeaked the mouse. "I . . . I didn't mean to disturb your sleep. Please don't harm me. If you spare my life, one day I'll save yours."

"Ha ha," laughed the mighty lion. "How can you help me? You amuse me, little mouse, and because you do, I'll let you go."

The mouse scurried off as soon as his feet reached the ground.

Many months went by, and the mouse kept as far away from the lion as possible. Then one day he heard the most pitiful moaning. He followed the sound, which led him to the lion, who was hopelessly tangled in a hunter's trap.

"Mr. Lion, sir," said the mouse, "a while ago I promised to repay your kindness. Today, I shall keep my word."

Right away, the mouse went to work gnawing at the ropes that held the lion. In no time, the lion was free.

"Mouse," said the lion, "I did not believe that the likes of you could ever rescue me, but now I know you are a true friend."

LITTLE FRIENDS MAY BECOME GREAT FRIENDS.

The Ass, the Fox,
and the Lion

After deciding to become partners, an ass and a fox went out into the country to hunt. On the way they met a lion. Realizing the danger ahead, the fox went straight to the lion and whispered, "If you promise not to harm me, I'll betray the ass, and you'll easily have him in your power."

The lion agreed, and the fox managed to lead the ass into a trap. No sooner did the lion capture the ass than he quickly attacked the fox and kept the ass in reserve for his next meal.

TRAITORS MUST EXPECT TREACHERY.

The Birds, the Beasts, and the Bat

Once upon a time there was a fierce war waged between the birds and the beasts. For a while the outcome of the battle was uncertain, and the bat, taking advantage of his ambiguous nature, kept out of the fray and remained neutral. Finally, when it appeared that the beasts would prevail, the bat joined their side and was active in the battle. The birds rallied successfully, however, and the bat was found among the ranks of the victors at the end of the day.

After a peace agreement was speedily concluded, the bat's conduct was condemned by both parties, and since he was recognized by neither side and thus excluded from the terms of the truce, he was compelled to skulk off as best he could. Ever since then he has lived in dingy holes and corners, never daring to show his face except in the dusk of twilight.

THOSE WHO PRACTICE DECEIT MUST EXPECT TO BE SHUNNED.

The Frogs
Who Desired a King

A long time ago, when the frogs led a free and easy life in the lakes and ponds, they became disgruntled because everyone lived according to his own whim, and chaos reigned. Consequently, they gathered together and petitioned Jupiter, the mighty god, to let them have a king who would bring order into their lives and make them more responsible. Knowing how foolish the frogs were, Jupiter smiled at their request and threw a log into the lake.

"There is your king!" he declared.

The log made such a splash that it terrified the poor frogs, who dove underwater and into the mud. No one dared to come within ten leaps of the spot where it lay in stillness. Eventually, one frog, who was bolder than the rest, ventured to pop his head above the water and watch their new king at a respectful distance. When some others soon perceived that the log was lying stock-still, they began to swim up to it and around it. At last they grew so bold that they leaped upon it and treated it with the greatest contempt.

Dissatisfied with such a tame ruler, they immediately petitioned Jupiter a second time to grant them a more active king. This time he sent them a stork, and no sooner did the bird arrive than he began seizing and devouring them one by one as fast as he could. Devastated by their new king, the frogs now sent a private message to Jupiter, beseeching him to take pity on them once more.

But Jupiter replied that they were being justly punished for their folly and that maybe next time they would learn to let well enough alone.

WHEN YOU DESIRE TO CHANGE YOUR CONDITION, MAKE SURE
THAT YOU CAN REALLY IMPROVE IT.